DISNEY
Tangled
The Series

TALES OF RAPUNZEL 2

Opposites
Attract

For Steven
—K.M.

Copyright © 2017 Disney Enterprises, Inc. All rights reserved. Published in the United States by Random House Children's Books, a division of Penguin Random House LLC, 1745 Broadway, New York, NY 10019, and in Canada by Penguin Random House Canada Limited, Toronto, in conjunction with Disney Enterprises, Inc. Random House and the colophon are registered trademarks of Penguin Random House LLC.

randomhousekids.com

ISBN 978-0-7364-3828-5 (trade) —
ISBN 978-0-7364-3829-2 (lib. bdg.)

Printed in the United States of America

10 9 8 7 6 5 4 3 2

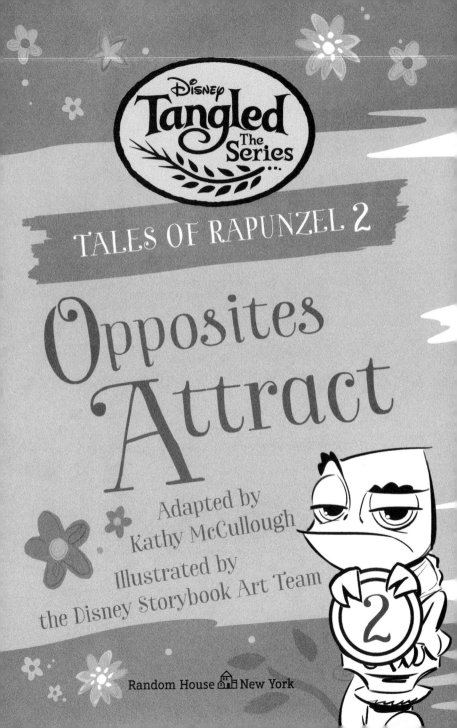

Disney

Tangled
The Series

TALES OF RAPUNZEL 2

Opposites Attract

Adapted by
Kathy McCullough

Illustrated by
the Disney Storybook Art Team

Random House 🏠 New York

Tale One

Cassandra
vs. Eugene

Rapunzel stood in her art studio, putting the final touches on her painting of a lighthouse. It had been a peaceful morning, sunny and quiet—just perfect for painting. Pascal sat on her shoulder, eyes closed.

Rapunzel was about to complete her final brush stroke, when—

"FITZHERBERT!"

Rapunzel's brush streaked across the canvas, ruining the painting.

"Ugh, not again," Rapunzel muttered to

herself. Cassandra's voice had come from a nearby room in the castle. Rapunzel knew what would happen next. Cassandra had shouted out Eugene's last name, which meant—

"I don't know what you're so upset about!" she heard Eugene yell. Pascal, awakened from his nap, covered his ears and shook his head in dismay.

Rapunzel sighed. Eugene and Cassandra were fighting.

Again.

As the argument continued, Rapunzel added her painting to a stack of several other ruined ones. This had happened before. Too many times. "This has got to stop," she told Pascal. He nodded.

Rapunzel found Cassandra and Eugene in the royal dining room. "Hey, guys!" she called out, keeping her voice light. "Everything okay? I couldn't help but overhear—"

Cassandra and Eugene went on fighting as if Rapunzel wasn't even there.

"Not only did you take my halberd without asking," Cassandra was saying, "you got your disgusting hair all over it!"

"I did *not* touch your halberd," Eugene insisted—then paused, looking confused. "Wait, what's a halberd?"

Cassandra held up a long pole with a large double-sided ax at the top. It was one of the many weapons she'd learned to use thanks to her father, the captain of the royal guard.

"Oh . . . a halberd," Eugene said. "Fine. You got me." He pointed to his face. "But check out this shave. Smooth as a baby's bottom." He patted his cheeks above his goatee.

Cassandra rolled her eyes. "More like a *monkey's* bottom."

"Come on, guys." Rapunzel stepped between the two of them before Cassandra could use the halberd against Eugene. "This is ridiculous!" Pascal, still on her shoulder, nodded in agreement. "Let's all take a calm, cleansing breath. . . ."

"To be fair," Eugene said, ignoring her, "I asked you several times if I could use that thing."

Cassandra glared at him. "And I said *no* every time! A halberd should only be handled by a skilled warrior."

Eugene snatched the halberd from Cassandra. "Flynn Rider has handled plenty of weapons."

He swung the halberd, not seeing the tall

vase at the edge of the dining room table until it was too late.

CRASH! The vase shattered as the halberd hit it.

Eugene's mouth dropped open in horror.

Cassandra let out a triumphant laugh. "Way to go, Eugene!" Eugene's cheeks turned red.

"Let's not panic," Rapunzel said, even though she *was* panicked. "I mean, it is—*was* my dad's favorite one-of-a-kind vase, but—"

"I have an idea," Cassandra told Eugene. "Why not just steal him another one? Oh, wait, you can't! Because it was one of a kind!" She smiled. "And it'll be the first thing the king sees when he sits down to dinner tonight—or rather, *doesn't* see."

Eugene scowled at her. "You *love* making me look like an idiot in front of the king, don't you?"

"Nope," Cassandra said. "You do a perfect job of that all on your own."

Cassandra and Eugene continued arguing. Rapunzel gave up trying to stop them.

"I can't take it anymore," she told Pascal as they left the dining room. "Why can't they just get along?"

Pascal shrugged.

The angry voices faded as Rapunzel and Pascal reached the end of the hall. "I bet they'd be great friends if they stopped fighting long enough to spend some quality time together," Rapunzel said. "Wait! That's it! I know how to fix this!"

Pascal glanced up at her, skeptical.

Rapunzel smiled. "We'll *make* them spend time together!"

Pascal crept down the castle hallway on a mission, a note clasped in his mouth.

He entered the kitchen. Cassandra sat near the hearth, sharpening a sword. She had changed out of her lady-in-waiting dress into the tunic, tights, and boots she wore for her guard training.

Cassandra looked up as Pascal approached

her. She took the note from his mouth. "What's this?" she asked him.

Pascal shrugged. He didn't wait for her to read the note. His mission was not yet complete. He had one more note to deliver—to Eugene.

Pascal found him in another part of the castle, talking to Stan, one of the guards. Pascal tapped Eugene's ankle to get his attention.

"Just a second, frog," Eugene said. "I'm busy."

Annoyed at being called a frog, Pascal flicked his long tongue up and slapped Eugene in the face. *That* got his attention.

Eugene took the note. "A note from Cassandra?" he said in surprise. "Hmm. This ought to be interesting. . . ."

The note instructed Eugene to meet Cassandra in one of the cells in the dungeon.

"It's a pretty grim place to offer an apology," Eugene told himself as he entered the cell. "But then again, this is Cassandra we're talking about."

Cassandra suddenly stepped out of the shadows. Eugene jumped, startled. "Did you just say *I* was going to offer *you* an apology?" she asked him.

Eugene held up his note. "Your note said to meet you here so you could tell me you were sorry."

"I didn't write you a note," Cassandra told him. "*You* wrote *me* a note."

Before Eugene could answer, the cell door slammed shut, locking them both in.

Outside the cell stood Rapunzel, with Pascal on her shoulder, a key in her hand, and a big grin on her face.

"Hey!" Eugene said. "What are you doing?"

"Time for the game to begin," Rapunzel said.

"Game?" Cassandra said. "What are you talking about?"

Rapunzel pressed the tips of her fingers together and gave Cassandra and Eugene a sly look. "Don't you see? *I* wrote the notes. It was just a trick to get you down here. The only way you can get out is by working together to solve the puzzle."

Rapunzel gestured to the dungeon cell. "Within these walls you'll find a series of clues. Put them together and you're free to go. Fail and this prison cell will become your new home." She let out a cackle, like a storybook villain, and strode down the hall toward the dungeon exit.

"Oh! I forgot," Rapunzel said, spinning around and running back. "I made you cookies!" She dropped a cloth-covered basket outside the cell before darting off again.

Eugene pouted and grabbed a cookie from the basket. He bit into it. "Mmm. Chocolate chip. My favorite."

He lifted the basket into the cell and lay down with it on one of the cots.

Cassandra didn't care about the cookies. She stood at the cell door and tugged on the bars. There was no way she wanted to be locked in with Eugene for another second, much less the rest of her life.

"This is all your fault," she said to him.

"My only fault is that I have no faults," Eugene replied as he bit into another cookie. He peered into the basket. "Hmm . . . all these delicious cookies and no milk? Wait, she did pack milk!" Eugene removed a bottle of milk from the basket and chugged it down, emptying it. "Ahh!" he said when he'd finished.

Cassandra marched over to him. Frustration had made her hungry. She saw the empty basket. "Did you eat all the cookies?"

"I'm not a pig, Cassandra," Eugene replied with a grin. "I ate all *your* cookies. I'm saving

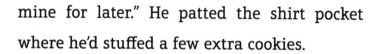

mine for later." He patted the shirt pocket where he'd stuffed a few extra cookies.

"Ugh! You're a selfish freeloader!"

"I could rattle off insults describing your personality, too," Eugene told her. "But that would imply you actually *have* one."

He was about to pop one of his saved cookies in his mouth when Cassandra grabbed it. "Don't eat that!" she said. She'd noticed something strange about it. "Let me see the others." She snatched the rest of Eugene's extra cookies from him. Half of them had "X6" written in icing on the top. The other half had "Y15."

"That's it!" Cassandra declared. Rapunzel hadn't left the cookies for them to *eat*. She'd left them because they were clues. "The cookies are the secret to getting out of here!"

A crumb from one of the cookies had fallen through a grate in the floor of Eugene and Cassandra's cell and landed on the floor of the cell below them.

Two hulking figures sat across from each other on cots inside the cell. One of the figures leaned down to pick up the crumb, and the light from the dungeon hall lit up his face.

It was Sideburns, one of the Stabbington brothers. He held the crumb between two fingers and cocked his head, listening to the voices above them.

The Stabbingtons were twin villains. Eugene

had been part of their gang back when he was a thief. The Stabbingtons, without Eugene, had tried to kidnap Rapunzel, but in the end, they were arrested—and they blamed Eugene.

"Recognize that voice?" Sideburns asked his brother, Eyepatch. "It sounds like our old friend Flynn Rider."

CHAPTER 3

Eugene leaned over Cassandra's shoulder, examining the coded cookies.

"These are coordinates for a grid," Cassandra said. "Rapunzel must've hidden the key to the cell behind a loose brick in the wall, and these cookies tell us which one."

Cassandra remembered from her math classes that x referred to a horizontal line across a grid, and y was the line that went up and down. She moved to the brick wall of the cell and counted six columns in from the

21

barred door. She then counted fifteen bricks up from the floor. The fifteenth brick was loose! In a second they'd be free!

Cassandra removed the brick and reached into the space behind it. She felt something metal, with a sharp end, but it didn't feel like a key. She pulled it out.

It was a rusty spring the length of her middle finger.

Eugene frowned. "That's it? That's no key."

"Wait, there's more," Cassandra said, reaching into the hole again. She grasped a piece of paper between her fingers and pulled it out. It was another clue. She read it aloud. "'This one is easy, just follow my lead.'"

Now Cassandra frowned. "Follow her lead? How? She locked us in here." She groaned. "This makes no sense."

Eugene spotted something on the floor near the rear wall of the cell. "That's because we're not supposed to follow her *lead*. We're supposed to follow her lead," he said, pronouncing it "led." He pointed to a pencil at the base of the wall. "Lead pencil," he explained. "Different words, same spelling."

Above the pencil was a drawing of an arrow, pointing to a small gear wedged into a crack in the cell's windowsill.

Eugene plucked the gear from the wall. "Aha!" he said.

"That's two clues so far," said Cassandra. "There must be more hidden around here."

She and Eugene worked together, searching every corner of the cell. They found two screws, a large hook, a short steel rod, and a flat piece of metal with two holes in it. Finally, under one

of the mattresses, they found a book with a hidden compartment containing a small comb.

"I've been looking for this!" Eugene grabbed the comb. He crossed to a piece of cracked mirror hanging on the cell wall and began to comb his hair.

Cassandra spotted a piece of paper at the bottom of the book's compartment. She unfolded it and read, "'This is your final clue,

so pick up the pace. You'll find the last treasure in the same spot you find your face.'"

Cassandra glanced around the cell. She was sure they'd searched everywhere, so where was the final piece to the puzzle?

Eugene grinned at his reflection in the mirror. "Looking good," he said to himself.

"Face . . . ," Cassandra murmured. She darted to the mirror and snatched it off the wall.

"I was using that!" Eugene protested.

Cassandra ignored him. She flipped over the mirror and found a cork taped to the back. "Another useless item," she said. She frowned and tossed it to the floor with the other mysterious bits and pieces of things they'd found.

Cassandra sighed, frustrated. They'd located all the clues and weren't any closer to getting out than when they'd started. They were still stuck in the cell, and with each other.

Cassandra and Eugene exchanged a worried look. Would they really be trapped in this dungeon forever?

Meanwhile, in the Stabbingtons' cell, Sideburns listened to the voices above them. He'd heard the name "Eugene" and remembered that it was Flynn Rider's real first name.

Sideburns was sure now: the man he wanted revenge on most in the world was directly above them, almost within reach.

Eyepatch had heard it, too. He paced the cell, grunting. Eyepatch was a man of few words— no words, really. He let his brother do all the talking. He used grunts and growls to express

his anger at being so close to Flynn Rider—and yet too far away to do anything about it.

Eyepatch banged his fists against the cell wall and let out a howl of rage.

"Patience, brother," Sideburns told him softly. "Our time will come. . . ."

CHAPTER 4

Rapunzel finished her new village painting and stood back to admire it. Pascal, on her shoulder, nodded in approval. "Listen," she said to him. "Do you hear that?"

Pascal cocked his head and listened. He didn't hear anything.

"That's the sound of peace and quiet," Rapunzel told him.

After locking her friends in the dungeon cell, Rapunzel had spent the rest of the morning in her studio. It was filled with projects she'd been able to finish in the hours since.

She'd knitted sweaters, sculpted pots out of clay, and strung banners. She'd built five birdhouses, assembled four dream-catchers, and baked a three-layer cake. It was amazing how much she could get done with no interruptions!

"Sticking those two together to work out their differences was one of the best ideas I've ever had," she said.

Pascal peered up at her doubtfully.

"Relax," she told him. "I'm sure they're doing just fine."

Cassandra and Eugene lay on their cots, staring at the ceiling. An awkward silence hung between them.

Finally, Eugene spoke. "So, Cass, tell me . . . what's your story? Other than that you're

a lady-in-waiting who knows how to use a halberd, I don't know the first thing about you."

"What do you want to know?" she asked.

"What are your hopes? Your dreams?"

"I don't have time for dreams," Cassandra said.

Eugene glanced over at her. "No time for dreams? You're hanging out with the *wrong* princess." They both knew Rapunzel was a dreamer, fueled by the wishes of all she hoped to do and see in the world.

"My dad taught me at a young age to focus on the here and now," Cassandra explained.

Eugene nodded. "Being raised by the captain of the guard must've been difficult."

"He's a good man," Cassandra said quickly. She loved her father. He'd taught her a lot over the years. "He showed me how to defend myself," she told Eugene. "How to take on responsibility and earn my keep—that's why I'm a lady-in-waiting." She paused as a pang of sadness came over her. "Besides, I don't remember my real parents, so I have nothing to compare him to anyway."

Eugene realized they had more in common than he thought. "I don't remember my parents, either," he told her. "I used to imagine they were explorers, searching the world for treasure, and that once they found it, they'd come back to the orphanage and get me." He let out a soft laugh. "Dumb, I know. How about you? Do you ever imagine what your parents were like?"

That was a question Cassandra didn't like thinking about. "I really don't want to discuss this with you, Eugene," she said sharply, rolling

over on her side to face the wall. "Stop trying to pry into my life."

"I wasn't prying," Eugene said, offended. "I was asking a simple— Wait a minute! That's it! *Pry!*" He jumped off the cot and dashed over to the items they'd found.

Cassandra sat up and looked down at him, confused.

"We're supposed to build a jack with this stuff," Eugene explained as he sorted through the odds and ends. "And use it to pry the door open!"

Cassandra joined him on the floor. Together they sorted through the pieces, putting them together one by one. When they finished, they had a tool that could be wedged between the cell door and its frame to pry the door open.

Cassandra snatched up the jack and darted to the door. She shoved one end of the jack into it, near the lock.

Eugene hurried over and grabbed the jack out of her hand. "You're not doing it right," he told her. "Leverage, Cassandra. It's all about leverage."

Eugene had learned about leverage during his years as a thief. Being able to use something small but strong,

like a sturdy stick or a thin metal bar, had come in handy when prying open locked doors. You use your strength to move the lever, but you also have to have the lever in the right spot, at the right angle. Even using a finger to open an envelope is a form of leverage. If your angle is wrong, you end up with a shredded envelope— and probably a paper cut, too.

Eugene was lining up the metal base of the jack with the door frame when Cassandra yanked it away from him again. "I know what I'm doing," she said. She hated when Eugene tried to act like he was so much smarter than she was.

"You *don't* know what you're doing," Eugene insisted, reaching for the jack.

"Cut it out!" cried Cassandra as she shielded the jack with her body.

"*You* cut it out!" Eugene replied. "The jack was my idea." He grabbed one end of it, but Cassandra refused to let go. They tugged back and forth.

"We wouldn't even have the jack if I hadn't stopped you from eating all the cookies!" Cassandra exclaimed.

As they each gave a final tug on the jack, it slipped from their hands, falling to the floor and shattering. The pieces rolled to the grate in the floor and fell through, lost forever.

CHAPTER 5

The Stabbington brothers watched as the screws and other parts fell from the ceiling to the floor in front of them.

Eyepatch helped Sideburns assemble the jack. They knew what the pieces were for, having overheard Cassandra and Eugene explain how to put them together.

When they'd finished, they stared at the jack, unsure what to do with it. The brothers had never used leverage to break into a building and steal. They'd always just bashed their way in.

Sideburns heard one of the castle guards approaching. He smiled.

When the guard arrived outside the cell, Sideburns reached his arm through the bars and bashed the guard over the head with the jack. The guard collapsed, unconscious.

Sideburns grinned. "Works like a charm." He grabbed the guard's keys and unlocked the door, then picked up the guard's halberd and handed it to Eyepatch. "Time for revenge," he said to his brother.

"Woo-hoo! I win!" Rapunzel shouted, throwing down the cards she was holding. She and Pascal loved playing all kinds of games—including cards.

Pascal, sitting across from her, lowered his

cards and frowned, then pointed to the clock next to him.

Rapunzel's smile faded. "You're right. It *has* been a long time. We should probably check on them." Pascal gave her a knowing look. "That doesn't mean my plan didn't work," she insisted.

With Pascal perched on her shoulder, Rapunzel headed to the dungeon. She hoped she was right and that she hadn't heard from Cassandra and Eugene because they were having too much fun with her game and had become friends.

That was what she hoped . . . but she had her doubts.

Eugene and Cassandra were sitting in their cell, feeling defeated.

Suddenly, they heard the door unlock. Eugene spun around. "Blondie!" he cried out. "Finally! Wh—"

It wasn't Rapunzel outside the cell.

"Hello, Rider," Sideburns said.

Cassandra glanced between Eugene and the hulking twins looming in the doorway. "I'm assuming these are friends of yours?" she asked him.

Eugene ignored her and gave Sideburns a big smile. "Sideburns!" he said. "You look great! Did you lose weight?" There was no answer

42

from either of the men towering over them. "Um . . . I guess not."

A whistle sounded in the distance and a voice cried out. "The Stabbingtons have escaped!"

Sideburns turned to his brother and glared. "I guess we're going to need a couple of human shields."

Before Eugene or Cassandra could react, Eyepatch had pulled sacks over each of their heads.

The next thing Cassandra and Eugene knew, they were being carried down the dungeon hallway over the shoulders of the brothers. Cassandra kicked and squirmed and tried to get free, but Sideburns had a tight grip on her.

Eugene knew it was foolish to fight. Right now, anyway.

Several guards appeared at the opposite end of the hall, and the Stabbingtons came to a stop.

The guards pointed their crossbows at the twins. "Hold it right there!" the captain of the guard called out.

Sideburns lifted Cassandra off his shoulder and set her down in front of him. When he snapped the sack off her head, the guard gasped in shock.

"Cassandra!" the captain exclaimed.

"Dad!" Cassandra wished she could run to her father—but Sideburns held on to her arm tightly.

Sideburns grinned. "I'd call your men off,

Captain, if you know what's good for your precious daughter."

At the same time, Rapunzel and Pascal had reached the entrance to the dungeon. "I hear voices," Rapunzel said with a smile. "It sounds like my plan worked."

She turned the corner—only to see the Stabbingtons holding Cassandra and Eugene hostage. Rapunzel hurried up behind the guards.

"Stay back, Princess," the captain warned her. He turned to his men. "Lower your weapons immediately." The guards reluctantly lowered their crossbows, and the Stabbingtons once again threw their captives over their shoulders. The brothers turned and quickly raced off in the opposite direction from the guards.

"Captain!" Rapunzel cried. "Hurry! They're getting away!"

Rapunzel knew that if the Stabbingtons reached the tunnel at the other end of the dungeon, they'd be able to get outside. Once they did, they could take off in any direction and the guards might never catch up to them.

Cassandra and Eugene would be gone forever.

Rapunzel and the guards chased the Stabbingtons and their captives. But the brothers were soon far ahead of them.

By the time Rapunzel reached the entrance to the tunnel, she couldn't see the guards anymore. She could only hear the echo of their footsteps, and she knew they couldn't catch up in time.

"Wait!" Rapunzel told Pascal. "Because of Cassandra, I know where this tunnel leads!" It was the same tunnel the girls had used to sneak out not too long ago. She spun around and ran back the way she'd come.

She only hoped it wouldn't be too late.

The Stabbingtons had gotten ahead of the guards, but Sideburns wanted to make sure they didn't catch up again. He noticed wooden beams crisscrossing the ceiling of the tunnel. There were also support beams attached along either wall. He tossed Cassandra to the floor, then kicked out one of the beams.

"Probably not the best idea," Eugene said, still hanging over Eyepatch's shoulder. But it was too late.

The fallen beam caused the ceiling to collapse, creating a wall of rock between the Stabbingtons and the guards.

Eyepatch dropped Eugene next to Cassandra.

"Say goodbye, you two," Sideburns said with a sneer. Eyepatch lifted the halberd over his head and was about to drop it on their captives when Sideburns grabbed his arm.

"Wait," he said. "I have a much better idea. We'll get rid of Rider and keep the captain's daughter as a bargaining chip."

Eugene scooted up against the rocks as the twins closed in on him. He tried to make a run for it, but Eyepatch grabbed him by the collar, dropping the halberd in the meantime. Behind the twins, Cassandra began to crawl quietly toward the weapon.

"Guys, hold on," Eugene said, putting his hands up. He noticed the support beam above Cassandra's head and got an idea. "Cassandra's useless," he continued. "I'm the one you want to take."

Cassandra had reached the halberd. As she quietly stood up, she saw Eugene glance her way.

"I'm the princess's boyfriend," Eugene went on. "I come with a lot more *leverage*." When Eugene said the word "leverage," he flicked his eyes up toward the beam in the ceiling over Cassandra's head.

"It ain't about leverage, Rider," Sideburns growled. As he moved in to grab Eugene, he didn't see Cassandra wedge the pole end of the halberd into the beam, disconnecting it from its supports on either side. Now only the force of the halberd held it up. "It's about revenge," Sideburns continued. "We've been waiting a long time for this."

Cassandra cleared her throat, and the twins turned toward her. As they did, she kicked the

halberd. It dislodged the beam, which fell right on top of the brothers, knocking them to the ground and trapping them.

Eugene grinned at Cassandra. "Now, *that's* how you use a halberd," he said.

"Yep," Cassandra agreed. "It's all about the leverage." They exchanged a smile.

Suddenly, the ceiling above Cassandra began to crumble. "Let's get out of here!" she cried.

Eugene and Cassandra raced away from the falling rocks, only to reach the end of the tunnel, which had already caved in.

They were trapped together again.

"Hello!" called a voice from above them. They looked up to see Rapunzel leaning in through a hole in the fallen section of the ceiling. Behind her, stars twinkled in the night sky.

Rapunzel let her long hair down through the hole until it reached them. As she pulled up her friends, the guards broke through the rocks and dragged the Stabbingtons out from under the fallen beam.

After the guards handcuffed the twins, the captain called up to Cassandra. "Are you okay?"

Cassandra glanced at Rapunzel and Eugene and smiled. "I am now," she said.

"I'm so sorry," Rapunzel told Eugene as they walked to dinner later that night. "I had no idea my game would lead to such a disaster. I really thought you guys would have fun."

Eugene shrugged. "You don't have to apologize. It must be hard for you with us fighting all the time. From now on, I'll try to be

nicer to the Dragon Lady—I mean, Cassandra."
Rapunzel smiled.

Eugene paused at the door to the dining room, suddenly nervous. "I can't believe I have to walk in there and tell the most important man in the kingdom that I broke his favorite vase." He dropped his face into his hands. "He's going to kill me."

"He's not going to kill you," Rapunzel said. "Even if that vase was the only one like it in the entire world."

"Not helping," Eugene told her.

Rapunzel bit her lip. "Sorry."

Eugene took a deep breath, pushed open the door . . . and froze.

The king and queen were already seated, and between them was the vase—completely repaired!

At the side of the room stood Cassandra, once again in her lady-in-waiting dress. Eugene spotted a jar of glue nestled in her palms. She smiled at him and he realized she had repaired the vase.

Rapunzel grinned. She knew her friends would be fighting again soon enough. But she had proven they *could* get along, and even help each other when it really mattered.

The End

Tale Two

In Like Flynn

During breakfast on the balcony one day, Rapunzel gazed down at the archway that led from the castle courtyard to the Corona town square. She loved being home after spending her first eighteen years locked in a tower. She wanted everyone who visited the castle to feel as happy as she did.

"Let's paint the archway," she suggested to her father. "Make it warm and welcoming." Rapunzel plucked a daisy from her long blond braid. "A flower design, maybe!"

Queen Arianna smiled, amused by her daughter's wish to spread joy to all corners of the kingdom. It was one of the many things she loved about her.

King Frederic loved his daughter, too. But he felt it his duty to teach her about the hard realities of the world.

"The archway is a major line of defense, Rapunzel," said the king. "It must demonstrate strength and security."

"You want strength and security?" asked Eugene, Rapunzel's boyfriend. "Two words: 'lion statue.' Better yet, turn the archway into a giant lion's mouth. Or—"

"Thank you, Eugene," said King Frederic. "I'll take those ideas under advisement."

"Great!" Eugene said. "It's all about the teamwork, am I right? Up high, Your Majesty!"

Eugene raised his palm for the king to give him a high five. The king didn't seem to notice and continued to eat his breakfast.

Eugene didn't care. He was pleased that the king liked his idea—and there were a lot more where that came from.

"You might want to draw some lion designs," Eugene told Rapunzel later that morning. "I can show them to your dad when I meet with him to discuss my great idea for redoing the archway."

They were in Rapunzel's art studio, where Rapunzel was painting a picture of her pet chameleon, Pascal. Pascal posed on a tiny sofa, a rose in his teeth.

"I'd wait on that, Eugene," said Cassandra, Rapunzel's good friend and lady-in-waiting.

"Whenever the king thinks an idea is dumb, he always says 'I'll take it under advisement.'"

Eugene was about to protest, until he remembered how many times the king had said those same words to him.

"This is awful!" he cried. "I can't have a father-in-law who doesn't take me seriously!"

Suddenly, a loud bell rang.

"The emergency alarm!" Cassandra shouted. The friends hurried to the castle entrance. They raced across the courtyard and through the archway into the town square.

In the middle of the square was King Frederic, scowling up at his statue. Black rings had been painted around its eyes, and several teeth had been blacked out. A sign around the statue's neck read EQUIS RULES!

Rapunzel stared at the sign, confused. "Isn't Equis the kingdom next door? What's it got to do with my dad's statue?"

The captain of the royal guard whispered to Rapunzel. "King Trevor, the ruler of Equis, is your dad's lifelong rival. He likes to play pranks on him."

"By drawing a silly face on his statue?"

said Rapunzel. "I can't imagine any intelligent person finding that funny." She was surprised to see Eugene trying not to laugh.

"King Trevor always manages to completely embarrass your father," the captain continued.

"I *am* embarrassed," King Frederic declared. "Embarrassed for *Trevor*! The idea of a *grown man* engaging in such childish behavior."

Eugene let out a snort of laughter. He couldn't help it! The eyes on the statue were pretty hilarious.

The king glared at him, and Eugene gulped back another laugh.

Rapunzel frowned. She was constantly surprised by how much she didn't know, having been locked in a tower for most of her life. "I still don't get it," she said.

"I'll explain later," Cassandra told her.

"Trevor has been trying to get me to partake in his shenanigans since our youth," said the king. "Well, I won't partake." He raised his fist toward the statue. "Do you hear me, Trevor?" he shouted. "I. Won't. Partake!"

Back in the castle, King Frederic slammed his fist on the arm of his throne. "I *must* partake!" he cried. "I must show the people of Corona that the sign is wrong! Equis does *not* rule!"

"I agree," said the captain of the guard. "But how?"

"I need a prank," said the king, smiling as an idea came to him. "I shall steal the thing Trevor holds dearest: the Seal of Equis, the very symbol of his land!"

The captain stared at the king in shock. "But, Your Majesty, the castle of Equis is impossible

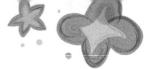

to break into. Only one man has ever slipped through its defenses!"

Just then, Eugene strolled past the open doorway of the throne room, whistling. He paused, sensing the stares of the king and the captain, who were looking his way.

Before giving up his life of crime for Rapunzel, Eugene had been a thief known as Flynn Rider. His success in breaking into King Trevor's castle was well-known. He'd only gotten away with a single silver candlestick, but the feat was impressive nonetheless.

Eugene didn't know this was why the king and the captain were staring at him, and he was a little worried. "What's going on?" he asked. "Are you guys talking about me?"

Eugene burst into the royal library. "Blondie!" he said to Rapunzel. "Guess what? Your dad asked me to steal the Seal of Equis!"

Rapunzel looked up from the book she was reading, which happened to be about Equis. "That doesn't sound like a good idea, Eugene," she said. She held open the book for him to see. "Did you know they have more than a thousand guards on duty at any one time?"

Pascal climbed from Rapunzel's shoulder to the top of the book. He turned the pages, pointing to the illustrations of the guards and the kingdom's many dungeon cells.

"I know all that." Eugene took the book and closed it, forcing Pascal to leap onto a nearby table. "But this is the perfect way to prove to your father that I'm more than just some nitwit thief."

Rapunzel gave Eugene a doubtful look. "You're going to prove you're not a thief by *stealing* something?"

"No. By stealing something *well*," Eugene explained. "It's for the official royal prank, so I'm pretty sure that makes it legal . . . ish."

"I'll come with you!" Rapunzel was determined to learn more about this whole "prank" thing.

Eugene shook his head. "Sorry, Blondie. This

is a one-man job." He grinned. "Luckily, Flynn Rider does his best work alone."

However, when Eugene stepped out of the castle archway later that day, he found King Frederic waiting. The king was dressed all in black and wore a satchel across his chest, exactly like the one Eugene was carrying.

"Let's go, partner!" the king said.

Eugene stared at him. "You want to come *with* me?"

"Of course!" replied the king.

"But I thought you wanted *me* to do it," Eugene said. *"Alone."*

"It's like you said before, Eugene—teamwork! How did you put it?" the king asked. "'Up high'?"

Eugene raised his hand to high-five, but King Frederic had walked away. He clearly

didn't understand what "up high" meant.

Eugene sighed. It seemed he was stuck with a partner, whether he liked it or not.

From a nearby hilltop, Eugene peered through his telescope at the castle of Equis. There were hundreds of guards patrolling the courtyard, just as he remembered, and just as it said in Rapunzel's book.

He lowered the telescope and turned to King Frederic, who was standing next to him. "I've come up with a plan based on the brilliant way I got into the castle before." Eugene showed the king a map he'd sketched of the castle. "First we'll need to steal a couple of uniforms from those guards down there, and then we'll go in through the front—"

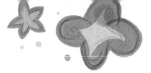

The king took the map from him. "We aren't doing that."

"Why not?" Eugene asked.

"As king, I received top military training," Frederic told Eugene. "What is required here is a stealthy ingress." The king noticed Eugene staring at him, confused. "In other words, we need to sneak in the back way." He placed his

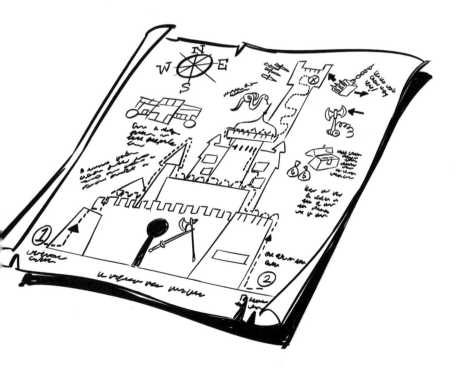

finger on the map. "And this is the perfect spot to do it."

"The Northeast Tower?" Eugene asked, surprised. "That's the most heavily guarded part of the whole castle!"

The king smiled. "No one will expect it!" he said. "But we'll need a disguise." He spotted a row of shrubs outside the castle walls. "Shrubberies!" he declared. "Perfect!"

While Eugene and King Frederic plotted their prank, Rapunzel was trying to figure out exactly what a prank *was*. She sat at her bedroom window, gazing down at the square, where guards were scrubbing the paint off the king's statue. "What's so fun about pranks anyway?" she asked Cassandra.

Cassandra glanced up from watering the

plants. "Mostly the look on the other person's face when they realize what's happened."

"Is a prank just a mean joke, then?" Rapunzel asked.

"A good prank isn't." Cassandra tried to come up with the best way to explain it. "It's like . . . You get somebody to expect one thing and then you do something *unexpected* instead."

"*Un*expected . . ." Rapunzel brightened, an idea taking hold in her mind. She tiptoed to Pascal, who was napping in his tiny bed on the nightstand. She gently set a sleeping mask over his eyes and covered him with a blanket.

Rapunzel whispered to Cassandra. "By the time Pascal wakes up, he'll be so well rested he won't know what hit him." She grinned. "I can't wait to see the look on his face!"

Cassandra shook her head. "Unexpected,

yes . . ." She snatched the sleeping mask off Pascal and his eyes popped open in shock. "But it has to be clever, too."

Outside the castle of Equis, King Frederic and

Eugene were cleverly disguised. At least, the *king* thought so.

"Follow my lead," he whispered. They were crouched inside a pair of large bushes that they'd pulled free from outside the castle wall.

The king moved his bush an inch to the right, waited a few seconds, then repeated the steps, inching his way through the courtyard toward the castle. Eugene had no choice but to follow.

Unlike the king, Eugene kept his eyes on the Equis guards. He knew that walking bushes—even if they moved very, *very* slowly—would look suspicious.

He was right. A nearby guard glanced their way and came over to investigate. Eugene quickly pulled the guard behind his bush, tied him up, and took his uniform.

The king noticed Eugene wasn't next to him and soon spotted him in the guard's uniform, striding toward the castle entrance.

"I thought I told you guard uniforms weren't necessary," he said sternly.

Eugene wanted to scream. This was so

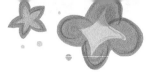

frustrating! *He* was the professional thief! He knew the best and fastest way to break into a castle. But even on *this* the king refused to take his advice!

Eugene couldn't disobey the king. But he really, really had to scream. Screaming out loud would surely get them caught, though, so he took off his helmet, ducked his face into it, and let out a yell. The helmet muffled the noise, and he felt a little better.

CHAPTER 3

"Ow!" Eugene yelled. "Agh! Ouch!"

"Quiet!" hissed King Frederic.

Eugene couldn't help it. Slamming into a brick wall was painful!

They'd reached the Northeast Tower without being caught and were now climbing to the top, using a rope the king had packed in his satchel. The king was above Eugene, and with every step he took, the rope swung out—and back—smashing Eugene into the wall.

Eugene was battered and bruised by the time they climbed through the window at the top of the tower. Once they were inside, however, he was determined to take charge. He knew the castle better than the king, and he was sure King Frederic would listen to him now.

Eugene slipped ahead and peeked around the edge of a corridor. Two guards were at the far end, but they soon turned and disappeared into a room.

The coast was clear.

"Okay," Eugene whispered. "Follow my—" Before he could finish, the king somersaulted across the hallway, grunting as he tumbled. The guards immediately heard the commotion and looked back in their direction.

Eugene snatched some coins from his pocket and tossed them high over the guards' heads. The coins clattered on the stone floor at

the opposite end of the hall. "This way!" one of the guards shouted. The guards dashed off, following the sound.

Eugene glanced ahead, expecting the king to compliment him on his quick thinking. But the king hadn't seen what he'd done.

"What are you doing back there?" King Frederic demanded, waving a hand over his head. "Follow my lead!"

Eugene gave up. It was only a matter of time before they were caught. He might as well do whatever the king wanted until that happened. . . .

Eugene wasn't the only one waiting to be caught. Rapunzel had spent all morning trying to come up with a prank. She thought about what the people in the castle *expected* to happen during the day and tried to figure out how to make one of those things turn out the opposite way.

That was how she ended up inside a large cabinet.

"Let's do this fast, so we can get to lunch," a voice said.

Rapunzel recognized the voice. It was Pete, one of the guards. A moment later, she heard another guard, Stan.

"You clean the spears," Stan said. "I'll work on the swords."

Rapunzel smiled, ready for her prank. She banged a fist on the inside of the cabinet and squinted through a crack in the doors. She saw the guards point their spears at the cabinet and creep toward it.

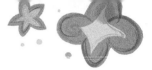

Just before the guards reached the cabinet, Rapunzel swung open the doors and leaped out, a sword in her hand.

"Gotcha!" she yelled. The guards screamed in fright.

Rapunzel raised her sword, gesturing to the inside of the cabinet. Rows of gleaming, polished swords and knives lined the cabinet walls.

"I cleaned all these weapons before you could!" she told the shocked guards. "You should see the looks on your faces!" She let out a gleeful laugh. "You've just been pranked—or as it will soon be called, *Rapunzeled*."

It was obvious to Rapunzel that she was already so good at this prank thing, they'd *have* to change the word to name it after her.

Stan, overcome by excitement, fainted. As Pete leaned down to check on him, Cassandra appeared in the doorway.

Rapunzel wasn't sure whether fainting was the normal reaction to a prank. She looked at her friend eagerly, ready for congratulations.

Instead, Cassandra shrugged. "That was clever," she admitted. "And unexpected . . ."

Rapunzel could sense a "but" coming—and she was right.

"But a great prank has to be funny, too."

Meanwhile, in Equis, Eugene was *not* finding anything to laugh about.

King Frederic tiptoed ahead of

him down one hallway, then another—twelve hallways so far. Eugene was beginning to suspect that the king was lost—even though he would wave and whisper "Follow my lead" at the end of each corridor before turning yet another corner.

Eugene had gotten so used to tiptoeing and turning corners that when the king suddenly stopped in front of a doorway, Eugene nearly ran into him.

"The royal seal room!" the king said with a smile.

The door was locked, but Eugene still had twigs stuck in his hair from hiding in the bush. He plucked one out and picked the lock. The king opened the door, and Eugene followed him inside.

At the far end of the room was a raised platform covered by a velvet curtain.

"Behind that curtain lies the royal seal of Equis," the king told Eugene, yanking the curtain aside.

Eugene stared. He was shocked, stunned, bewildered . . . and speechless.

Sitting atop the platform was a seal. Not the silver or brass kind, with the image of the kingdom stamped on it. This was a *seal*. A live, whiskered, blubbery sea mammal-type seal. The kind that lived in the ocean—or *should*, anyway.

"Arf!" barked the seal.

CHAPTER 4

"It's a seal," Eugene said, once his power of speech had returned.

"Indeed," the king declared. "The royal seal!"

"It's a *seal* seal," protested Eugene. "Not a royal seal."

"It's a *seal* seal owned by a king," the king explained. "And thus a royal seal."

Eugene considered pointing out how ridiculous it was for King Trevor to have a marine creature as a "royal seal," but it wasn't worth the time. They needed to get out of the castle with the animal before they were caught. "Just grab one end and let's go," he told the king.

Instead, King Frederic crossed the room to a portrait of King Trevor on the wall. He took a paintbrush from his satchel. "What should I paint?" he asked Eugene. "An eye patch? Some stink lines? A tear representing Trevor's embarrassment when he realizes I've outpranked him?"

"None of those things!" cried Eugene. "We've got to go—*now!*" He threw out his arms in frustration, accidentally slapping the seal. The creature let out a loud "ARF!" in response.

A second later, footsteps sounded from the hallway.

Eugene looked around for an escape. He glanced at the ceiling and got an idea. "I'm going to need your rope," he told the king.

When the guards stormed in a few seconds later, Eugene, the king, and the seal were gone.

Or at least, they *seemed* to be gone. They were actually hiding in the chandelier, which dangled over the guards' heads.

As the guards searched the room, King Frederic whispered to Eugene, "What're we going to do?"

Eugene stared at the king in disbelief. "*Now* you want my advice?"

"You're the expert," said the king.

"That's what I tried to tell you from the start!"

As they argued, the chandelier swayed. The bolts connecting it to the ceiling twisted loose and fell to the floor one by one. Suddenly, the chandelier broke free—crashing to the ground!

The guards surrounded Eugene and the king, spears pointed at the two burglars.

"Arf!" barked the seal.

"Well," said the king. "It seems this prank has gone horribly wrong."

King Frederic slumped sadly next to Eugene inside a dark dungeon cell. Eugene felt sorry

for him. Eugene himself had made lots of mistakes during his time as a thief, and he knew how bad it felt. But he imagined it must feel much worse to be a *king* and mess up.

"I'm sorry I lost my temper," he told the king. "It's just that this was my chance to get you to take me seriously for once."

King Frederic stared at Eugene, surprised. He hadn't thought much about Eugene's feelings during this whole adventure. He'd been too focused on embarrassing Trevor.

"You brought my daughter home to me after eighteen long years," the king told him. "If there's one man in the whole world I take *very* seriously, it's you."

Eugene was amazed. King Frederic didn't think he was just some nitwit thief—he actually had respect for him!

"Thanks, Your Majesty," he said. "May I ask then why you *didn't* listen to my ideas when we were breaking into the castle?"

The king sighed. "Sometimes I let good ideas slip through the cracks. I should have given your plan a chance."

"What you *should* have done was stayed in your own kingdom, Frederic," a voice called.

Eugene and King Frederic looked up to see King Trevor standing in the dungeon hallway, holding the seal tightly on a leash. The seal stared at Eugene and King Frederic with a sad expression and tears in its eyes.

King Trevor sneered at the prisoners. "Your efforts to steal Trevor, Jr., were comical at best."

"Your seal doesn't look too happy," Eugene observed.

King Frederic stood and faced King Trevor

through the bars of the cell. "All right, Trevor. You've had your laughs," he said. "Now release us."

"I'll let you go," replied King Trevor. "But not until I parade you through town wearing nothing but a jester's hat—proving once again that Equis is superior to Corona! Until then, I'm leaving you here to stew in the stench of your own defeat!"

King Trevor cackled as he yanked on the seal's leash, dragging the poor animal after him.

King Frederic plopped onto the cot and sighed. "Trevor's right," he said.

"You don't smell that bad, Your Majesty," Eugene assured him. "Besides, the stench in here is mostly from the seal. It's all that fish they eat."

"I *meant* I deserve to wear nothing but a jester's hat," said the king. "Once again, Trevor has proven he's the better prankster."

"*Better?*" replied Eugene. "His prank with your statue wasn't even funny! I mean, I laughed a *little*. But still. On the whole? Not that funny."

The king nodded. "True. His pranks are always more grating than humorous."

"Grating . . . ," Eugene murmured to himself.

"It means 'annoying' or 'irritating' or—"

"No, no," Eugene said. "*Grating*—that's how we get out of here!" He pointed to a grate in the floor of the cell. "The question is, are you willing to try it *my* way this time?"

CHAPTER 5

"Your Majesty! There's no way you'll escape *that* way!"

The two guards posted outside the dungeon door heard Eugene call out. They rushed into the dungeon and dashed to the cell to find Eugene alone.

"The king escaped without me!" Eugene told the guards, pointing to the floor of the cell. The grate was gone.

The guards hurriedly unlocked the cell door to investigate. They leaned down and peered into the hole in the floor.

"Lose something?" called a voice.

The guards glanced around, confused. The voice hadn't come from below. They looked up just as King Frederic, who had been hiding in the rafters, jumped on top of them, knocking them to the ground.

Eugene helped the king up off the dazed guards. "Well played, Your Majesty," he said with a smile. "Well played."

Back at the castle of Corona, things were also looking up for Maximus, a horse in the royal guard. Max was drinking from his trough when he spotted an apple on the ground nearby. It had appeared out of nowhere—as if by magic! Apples were Max's favorite.

He didn't notice the string attached to it and was about to

bite down on the apple when it darted out of his reach. Max followed the apple as it rolled toward the open doors of the stable barn.

Inside the barn, the apple came to a stop near a pile of hay. At last! Max opened his mouth wide ... and bit into nothing. The string had yanked the apple into the shadows.

The barn doors crashed closed behind him. Max looked around nervously as footsteps thundered above him.

Suddenly, Rapunzel jumped from the rafters to the hay-strewn ground. "Gotcha!" she cried.

Max watched, confused, as Rapunzel dashed around the barn, yanking down the curtains covering the walls. When she was done, Max stared in shock.

Towers of apples lined the barn. In front of one wall stood a sculpture of a horse made entirely of apples. It was Max's dream come true!

Rapunzel laughed and pointed at him. "You should see the look on your face!"

Max galloped straight into the sculpture and bit an apple. It was delicious!

Rapunzel left Max in the barn to gobble up the apples. Outside, Cassandra leaned against a wall.

"Did you see the look on his face?" Rapunzel asked her. "He expected one apple, but he got a whole bunch!" She grinned. "Best. Prank. *Ever!* He was totally Rapunzeled!"

Cassandra nodded. "Unexpected, clever, and funny. But there's one more thing a great prank has to be. . . ."

Rapunzel frowned. What could be left?

Cassandra smiled. "A prank has to be *mischievous*, too," she said.

Eugene and King Frederic hadn't carried out a great prank, either. But that was about to change.

They had locked the two guards in the cell and taken their uniforms. The disguises had been Eugene's original plan to get them *inside* the castle without being caught. Now he hoped the disguises would get them *out*.

Unfortunately, as Eugene and the king headed toward the castle entrance, King Trevor appeared at the opposite end of the hall.

King Frederic turned to go back the way they'd come, but Eugene grabbed his arm.

"Wait," he whispered, recognizing the hall from when he'd broken in before. "Follow my lead. . . ."

Before the king could answer, Eugene dashed to a door and rattled the handle. The king followed. Eugene looked over at the king and winked just as King Trevor marched toward them, dragging Trevor, Jr., on his leash.

King Frederic was confused. Was it Eugene's plan to get caught? But the king decided to trust him this time, and he hurried to Eugene's side.

King Trevor arrived beside them. "It appears *someone* hasn't learned their lesson yet," he said.

Eugene threw his hands up in surrender. "You got us!"

King Frederic slowly raised his hands as well, although he wondered now if trusting Eugene had been a mistake. Playing along, he said, "We wanted to pull off *some* sort of prank so our trip wasn't completely in vain."

Eugene added, "I thought it'd be funny to break into the library and rearrange the newspapers. Historians hate that."

King Trevor rolled his eyes. "That is the worst idea for a prank I've ever heard! And once again, you'd have failed!" He pointed to the door across the hall. "*That* is the door to the library!"

Eugene shook his head. "I'm pretty sure *this* is the library," he said.

"You idiot! This is *my* castle!" exclaimed King Trevor. "I know where my own library is!" He pushed Eugene and King Frederic aside, threw open the door, and stepped inside—right onto a trapdoor.

The trapdoor snapped open and Trevor plummeted out of sight with a scream.

Eugene called down through the opening. "Forgot about your own top-notch security, did you?"

CHAPTER 6

King Trevor yelled up from inside the trap. "Let me out, Frederic! There are spiders down here! *Ach!* One just touched me!"

King Frederic chuckled. He nodded to Eugene, impressed. "Well played, Eugene. Well played." The king raised his hand in the air, palm facing out. "Up high," he said.

Eugene hesitated, but this time the king kept his hand up. Eugene smiled and slapped King Frederic's hand.

The seal clapped his fins.

"Trevor, Jr., are you clapping?" King Trevor called. "Those better be claps of sorrow." The seal grinned and clapped harder.

King Frederic smiled at Eugene. "At last! I've finally humiliated Trevor."

"Oh, Your Majesty," Eugene said with a grin. "We have not yet *begun* to humiliate that guy."

All the way home to Corona, Eugene and King Frederic laughed, remembering how they'd tied King Trevor to the leg of his own statue in the Equis town square. They'd left him wearing nothing but a jester's hat—and a sign covering his body that read CORONA RULES!

The captain of the guard met Eugene and the king outside the Corona castle gates.

"Did you do it, Your Majesty?" the captain asked. "Did you get the seal?"

"We got him, Captain," the king replied. "But we let him go." He explained how they'd traveled to the seaside after leaving Equis and set Trevor, Jr., free.

"It's been an *excellent* day," the king declared as they neared the castle archway.

But then he saw it. . . .

The arch's gray stones had been painted pink and purple, and the whole structure was covered with pictures of daisies and birds.

"I guess we're not going with the lion theme," observed Eugene.

"I might have preferred it," replied the king.

Rapunzel popped out from behind the archway, a big grin on her face. "Gotcha, Dad!"

She
laughed. "Oh
man, you should *see*
the look on your face!"
The king chuckled. He
was in a good mood from
succeeding with his prank. It
was only fair that he allow his
daughter one of her own.
"I suppose it's fine," he
told her. "As long as you and
Cassandra repaint it—*today*."
Rapunzel held up
two cans of gray paint.
"Obviously, Dad," she said.

After the
king and Eugene
went inside, Cassandra
joined Rapunzel and
picked up a paintbrush.
"Well, Raps," she said. "You
finally figured out this whole
prank thing."

Rapunzel grinned from ear
to ear.

Cassandra smiled. "It was
unexpected, clever, funny, *and*
mischievous. But you overlooked
the most important part
of any prank:

You didn't think it through." She tossed a paintbrush to Rapunzel. "Now we have to repaint this whole thing by tonight."

Rapunzel handed the brush back to Cassandra. "Sorry, but I've got princess duties. Looks like you'll have to repaint it by yourself. Still believe I didn't think it through?" She snickered and skipped off toward the castle.

Cassandra stared at the paintbrush in her hand, then up at the huge stone archway—which would take *hours* to repaint by herself.

She groaned.

"Kidding!" a voice called from behind her. "I'm going to help you!" It was Rapunzel. She pointed a finger at Cassandra. "I totally got you, Cass! You should have seen the look on your face!" Rapunzel laughed as she picked up her paintbrush.

Cassandra shook her head. "I've been Rapunzeled," she said. Rapunzel giggled.

Cassandra dipped her brush in the paint and went to work next to Rapunzel. "Well played, Raps," she said with a sly smile. "Well played."

The End

Find out what happens next by reading more
TALES OF RAPUNZEL
adventures!

Don't miss book #3:
Friends and Enemies